# The GREAT MIGRATION

## JOURNEY TO THE NORTH

To my grandniece, Valerie Best,

for her lovely spirit and the joy she finds in using her talents

—E.G.


To my twin nieces, Morgan and Marion

With love, Auntie Jan

Amistad is an imprint of HarperCollins Publishers.

The Great Migration: Journey to the North
Text copyright © 2011 by Eloise Greenfield
Illustrations copyright © 2011 by Jan Spivey Gilchrist
Printed in the United States of America.

For information address HarperCollins Children's Books, a division of HarperCollins Publishers, 10 East 53rd Street, New York, NY 10022.
www.harpercollinschildrens.com

Library of Congress Cataloging-in-Publication Data
Greenfield, Eloise.
    The Great Migration : journey to the North / by Eloise Greenfield ; illustrated by Jan Spivey Gilchrist. — 1st ed.
        p.      cm.
    ISBN 978-0-06-125921-0 (trade bdg.) — ISBN 978-0-06-125922-7 (lib bdg.)
    1. African Americans—Migrations—History—20th century—Juvenile poetry.   2. African Americans—History—1877–1964—Juvenile
poetry.   3. African Americans—Southern States—History—20th century—Juvenile poetry.   4. Children's poetry, American.   I. Gilchrist, Jan
Spivey, ill.   II. Title.
PS3557.R39416G74   2011                                                                                                          2008043821
811'.54—dc22                                                                                                                              CIP
                                                                                                                                          AC

12  13  14  15      LPR      10  9  8  7  6  5
❖
First Edition

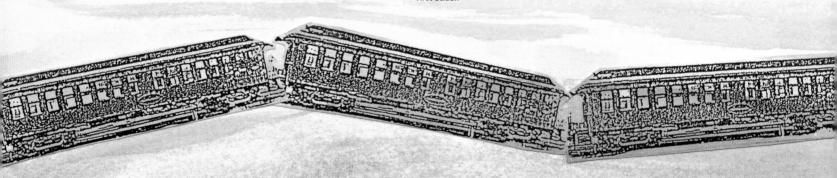

# The GREAT MIGRATION
## JOURNEY TO THE NORTH

By

### ELOISE GREENFIELD

Illustrated by

### JAN SPIVEY GILCHRIST

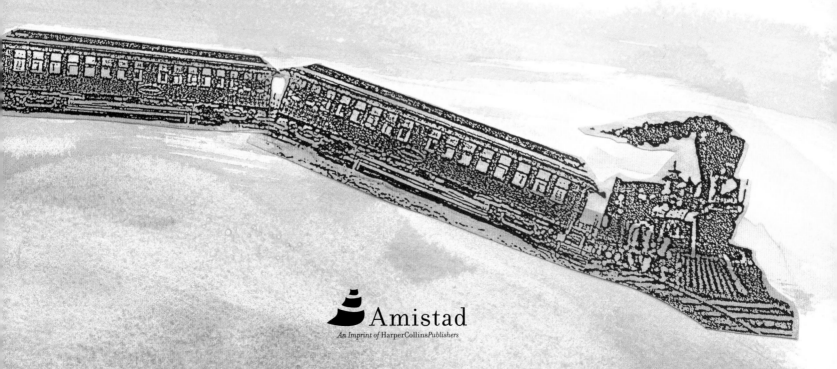

Amistad

*An Imprint of HarperCollinsPublishers*

**B**etween 1915 and 1930, more than a million African Americans left their homes in the South, the southern part of the United States, and moved to the North. This movement was named the "Great Migration."

In the South, members of the Ku Klux Klan were attacking African Americans, making it unsafe for them to live there. There were "White Only" signs on water fountains, in lunchrooms, and other places, meaning that only white people could use them. Many African Americans could not find jobs in the areas where they lived. For all of these reasons, African Americans, in large numbers, began to move away.

When they reached the North, they found that it was far from perfect. They had not escaped racial discrimination. Even so, things were better, and most people stayed in their new cities and worked hard to earn a living and take care of their children.

In August of 1929, when I was three months old, my father took the train northward from our home in Parmele, North Carolina, to Washington, D.C. My parents had heard from relatives and friends who had already moved to Washington how much better life was for them. Although Washington was not quite in the North, many North Carolinians and other southerners settled there.

My father found a job and a place for us to live. A month later, after he had saved enough money for train fare, he sent it to us, so that my mother, my brother, and I could join him. I was too little to know it then, but I had become a part of the Great Migration.

# I. The News

They read about it, heard
about it, in letters and newspapers
sent down from the North,
from visiting cousins and brothers
and aunts: there were jobs up there,
nice houses, no Ku Klux Klan
everywhere you turn, burning down
schools and homes and hope.
They thought about it, talked about it,
spread the word. "Did you hear the news?
Can it really be true? Well, I'm going
to see. How about you?"

## II. Goodbyes

### Man:

Saying goodbye to the land
puts a pain on my heart.
I stand here looking at the green
growing all around me,
and I am sad.
But I keep hearing about this
better life waiting for me,
hundreds of miles away,
and I know I've got to go.
Hope my old car can make it
that far.

## Girl and Boy:

I almost cried, having to tell
my friends goodbye. But
tomorrow, I'll get to hug
my daddy when I get off the train
up North. Mama says he found a job
and a place for us to live. *Up North.*
I wonder what it's like. Anyway,
as long as Mama and Daddy
are there, I know I'm going
to be happy.

## Woman:

I can't wait to get away.
I never want to see this town
again. Goodbye, town. Goodbye,
work all day for almost no pay,
enemy cotton fields, trying
to break my back, my spirit.
Goodbye, crazy signs, telling me
where I can go, what I can do.
I hear that train whistling
my name. Don't worry, train,
I'm ready. When you pull
into the station, my bags and I
will be there.

# Very Young
# Woman:

What should I pack?
Should I take everything,
in case I can't get back
anytime soon? I'm a little scared.
I'm a lot scared. Off to the
big city by myself, with just
the church up there to lean on.
Mama's making me go.
She wants me to be happy
and safe. But I see the sadness
lying deep in her eyes.
When she thinks I'm not looking,
she puts my teddy bear in the bottom
of the suitcase.
She knows I'm going to need it

# III. The Trip

Mostly they travel by train,
sit or stand in the railroad stations,
crowds of people, waiting,
resting their old suitcases,
cuddling their babies, holding the hands
of the older children, carrying,
in bags and shoe boxes,
food they've packed for the trip.

They hear the whistle blow.
It blows again, not so far away now.
They see the train coming closer
and closer, and then it stops. They gather
on the platform, hold out their tickets,
climb aboard. "All aboard!"
the conductor calls. It's time.
They're moving slowly,
then faster, some think too fast,
some think not fast enough,
toward a world they don't yet know.

At each station stop, more passengers
squeeze on until the train is full.
The children like to sit
beside a window and watch
the towns go by, watch the shapes
of trees, the fields of tobacco
and cotton and corn and beans.
The grown-ups talk, the children talk.
They laugh. They make new
traveling friends whom they
will never see again.

They watch the towns.
They watch the fields.
They think about the places they left.
They daydream about the places
they're going to.
*Going to Chicago, New York,*
*Philadelphia, Washington,*
*Pittsburgh, Cleveland, Detroit . . .*
and more.

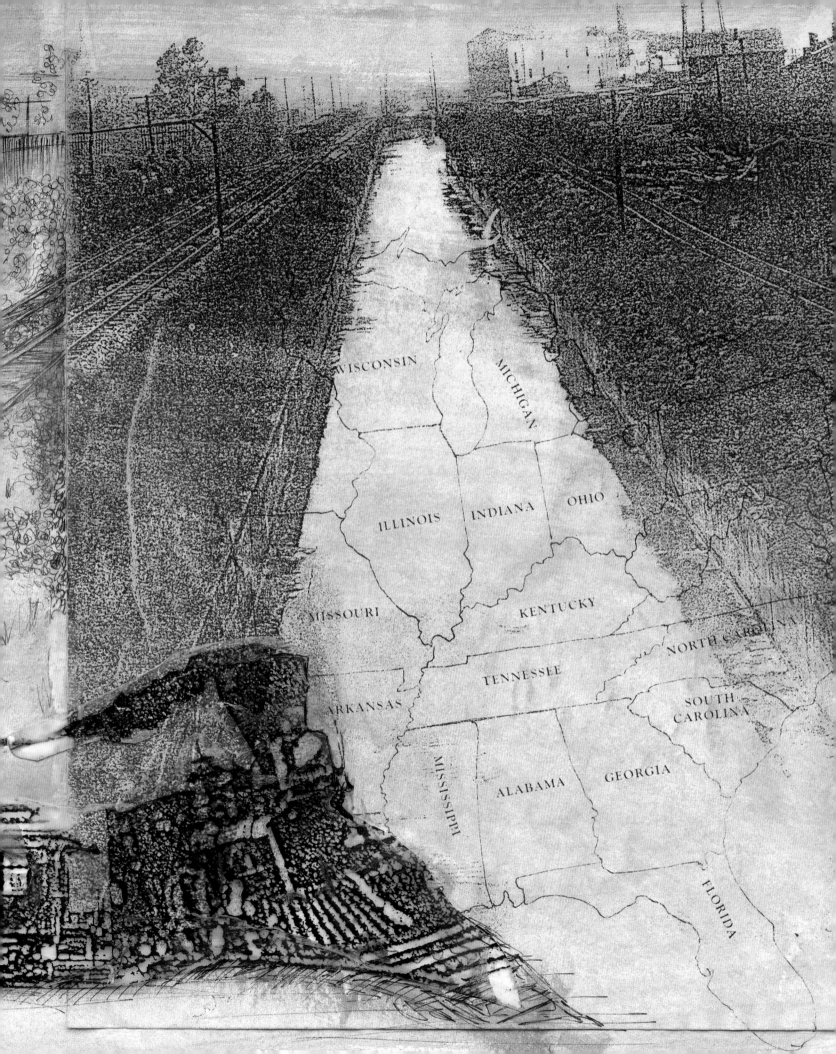

Night. Nothing to see in the darkness,
except the stars. And a little piece of moon.
Or maybe a big round one.
The same moon, the same stars
shine in their new cities.
They fall asleep. A baby tries
to cry, but sleep catches him
in the middle of his complaint.
Daylight. It's morning.
A long trip. Almost there now.
A new life is about to begin.

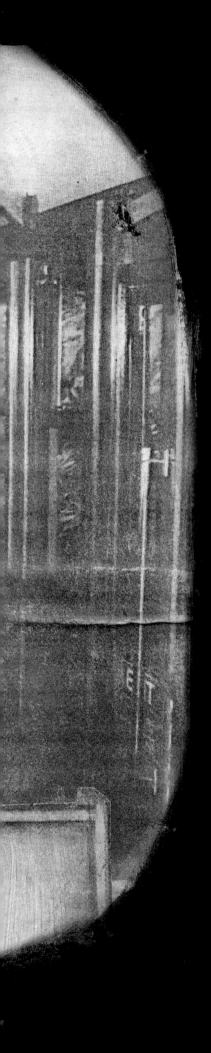

## IV. Question

## Men and Women:

Will I make a good life
for my family,
for myself?
The wheels are singing,
"Yes, you will,
you will, you will!"
I hope they're right.
I think they're right.
I know they're right.
We're going to have
a great life. Got to try it.
Going to do it. Going to
make it. No matter what.

# V. Up North

In the stations, they greet their
husbands, aunts, uncles, cousins,
friends who have come to welcome them,
show them the way toward
their future. In a few months,
*they* will be the ones guiding
newcomers, who will guide other
newcomers, who will guide . . .
and so on and so on and so on,
because the people keep coming,
keep coming, keep on coming,
filling up the cities with
their hopes and their courage.
And their dreams.

## My Family:

Parmele, North Carolina.
Nice town. Not many jobs, though,
in 1929. Not enough work
for Daddy, a man with a wife
and two children.
Some people were moving north.
Mama and Daddy read about it,
heard about it, from cousins
and friends. "Come north," they said.
"Come to Washington, D.C."
August. Mama and Daddy
wait at the station for Daddy's train.
Sad to separate, even for a little while.
Maybe longer. Who knows?
They say goodbye, but Mama
doesn't cry. Yet. She walks
the road home, alone. Sits on the
porch and lets the tears fall.

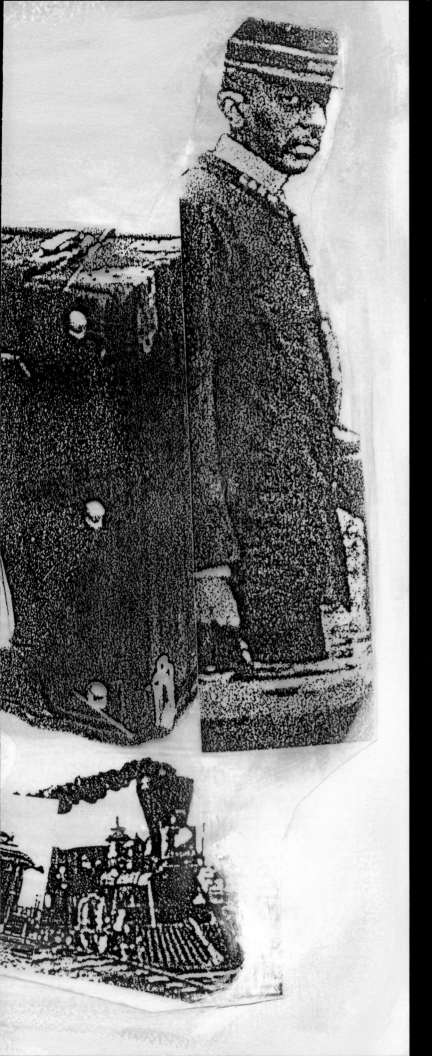

One long month and the money
comes. Train ticket money.
Daddy's found a job and a place
for us to live. "All aboard!"
the conductor calls. Not an easy trip
for Mama. Two babies to care for.
Me, four months old, my
big brother, Wilbur, eighteen
months. A long ride, and then,
"Wash-ing-ton!" the conductor
calls. We're home.

We were one family
among the many thousands.
Mama and Daddy leaving home,
coming to the city, with their
hopes and their courage,
their dreams and their children,
to make a better life.

# SELECTED BIBLIOGRAPHY

Bennett, Lerone, Jr. *Before the Mayflower: A History of the Negro in America 1619–1964.* Rev. ed. Baltimore: Penguin Books, 1966.

Candaele, Kerry. *Bound for Glory: From the Great Migration to the Harlem Renaissance, 1910–1930.* New York: Chelsea House, 1996.

Franklin, John Hope, and the editors of Time-Life Books. *An Illustrated History of Black Americans.* New York: Time-Life Books, 1970, 1973.

Lemann, Nicholas. *The Promised Land: The Great Black Migration and How It Changed America.* New York: Knopf, 1991.

Marks, Carole. *Farewell—We're Good and Gone: The Great Black Migration.* Bloomington: Indiana University Press, 1989.